Praise for *Tacoma*

"A charming story of coupling and nostalgia. This airy romance, much like its summer-home setting, is both beautifully constructed and packed with secret rooms. *Tacoma* feels like a new Burch era, though it's packed with plenty of what I've always loved. As always, Burch's self-assured prose shines."
—Amelia Gray, author of *Isadora*

"Aaron Burch's *Tacoma* is a shape-shifting feat of pure magic. It's a book about friendship and love and the moments in life that lift you up so you can see just how perfect and strange it all is. Big-hearted, playful, ironic, and yet somehow also strikingly sincere, this is the kind of book you read straight through, all the while hoping it will never end."
—Colin Winnette, author of *Users*

Tacoma

Aaron Burch

Autofocus Books
Easton, Pennsylvania

Published by Autofocus Books
autofocusbooks.com

Fiction/Literature
ISBN: 978-1-957392-45-5
Library of Congress Control Number: 2025951030

Portions of this book previously appeared, in various forms, in *Jake, Autofocus, Pool Party, Blue Stem,* and *X-R-A-Y.*

Cover design by Amy Wheaton

"Most days in Seattle are grey, but now I remember only the sunny ones."

—Denis Johnson, "Happy Hour"

TABLE OF CONTENTS

The house was hard to believe. Bigger, nicer, *everythinger* than anywhere either of us had lived. Anywhere either of us had imagined we'd be able to live. Probably anywhere you've imagined yourself able to live.

Beautiful mid-century modern, recently remodeled, state-of-the-art everything. A *Lifestyles of the Rich and Famous* episode devoted to a Frank Lloyd Wright house built in a waking life dream set in 21st century Pacific Northwest.

But the real showstopper was the view. The view! A wall of windows looked out at a fantasy novel's description of Tacoma—watercolor washes of blues accented with sparkling white caps of choppy water of the Puget Sound; a landscape of evergreen trees on the islands and land on the other side; above it all, the shaky seismograph readout of the Olympic Mountains capped with snow. I was reminded how much bigger and warmer and healthier my heart felt being near water, trees, mountains. How much more alive and open to the world.

It looked like a postcard. Like a single perfect shot from a movie. Like my nostalgic heart spilled out on canvas and come alive.

I guess I'll tell you now too, because I'm afraid starting with these too-good-to-be-true descriptions is setting up an expectation that it all went to shit. That the house was haunted or cursed. That we somehow ruined it, or over the course of the summer, it ruined us. That any story that starts with a feeling like living inside a dream has to turn into a nightmare.

That isn't this story though.

This is a story about magic and beauty and wonder.

Amber had a coworker, Eric, whose sister-in-law, Rachel, had an old sorority sister, Jessie, who had a cousin, Richie, whose hairstylist, Jesse, had a dogwalker, Arthur, who kept in touch with this guy, Georgie, who he'd used to work with at a hospital, and who, quote-unquote, *knows a guy*, whose parents, Ted and Alice, were looking for someone to housesit for the summer while they went to Europe.

I got confused midway through, trying to make sense of who knew who knew who knew who knew who, even though that wasn't even the point. But I'd gotten so lost, I'd missed the point.

I asked Amber to remind me, to go through it again, a little slower.

Amber went through it again, a little slower. This time, I wrote it all down, so I wouldn't get confused, and also because I like writing things down. Writing things down makes everything make sense. Makes everything more real.

OK, I said, after she'd gone through it all again and I'd written it all down so I wouldn't get confused, which also made it make sense and become more real.

Oh yeah! Amber said, like she'd forgotten. It's in Tacoma! Amber added, having very much not forgotten.

I grew up in Tacoma. Whenever I talked about it, it was like I was casting a spell, and I knew it was a spell of nostalgia, of a too-rosily-remembered childhood and stories retold until they'd become myth. But then the first time Amber and I visited, she fell in love with its magic too, and maybe it wasn't all and *only* too-rosily-remembered nostalgia.

Supposedly it has this amazing view of the Puget Sound and the Olympic Mountains and Mount Rainier and everything, Amber added.

We should house sit! I said. Like a joke, but also meaning it.

We should! Amber said. I couldn't tell if she was returning the joke or also meaning it or some secret third thing.

Amber worked for some kind of financial company. Or something like that. I'd know for sure and be able to explain it better if numbers and money weren't such a mysterious, indecipherable foreign language. What that meant though was that her job was work-from-home, and what *that* meant was that she could spend her dayjob hours anywhere, long as they were in front of a computer.

And I was a professor. Which meant I had summers off, which meant I could spend most of May through August anywhere, in front of a computer or not.

All of which meant there was no reason why we couldn't spend our summer in Tacoma, housesitting for Amber's coworker's sister-in-law's old sorority sister's cousin's hairstylist's dogwalker's old coworker's *guy he know*'s parents.

Our joking interest got game-of-telephone'd back as a sincere offer—or maybe the interest was sincere and the offer was joking, or maybe both, or neither, or maybe it's all the same thing—and because Ted and Alice were that hard-pressed for a housesitter or so carefree as to roll with any idea offered, or because they have a funny sense of humor or they were just calling our bluff, or their lives were so blessed that they always said yes to whatever the universe presented them, or, like us, they were so shocked the info not only made its way all the way to us but also all the way back to them, they took it as a sign—from God or the universe or whatever explanation they gave thanks to when a mystery of the world was answered with a solution— and they said sure.

And that's how we came to spend the summer in Tacoma.

A Little More About the House, Now That We'd Started to Get Settled (& Also a Confession About Wanting to Write a Great American Novel (GAN))

An adjustable height desk! I yelled to Amber, walking into the room that would become my temporary summer office.

Oh great, Amber said. Now you're definitely going to want one when we get home.

She was right. I definitely would.

A few months before this, during one of our Costco visits, an adjustable height desk had caught my eye. I'd never seen it there before. A new item. Or maybe we just didn't normally go down that aisle.

That's going to be my next big purchase, I'd said. It didn't even cost that much, but it was more than I let myself justify as a normal, not-big purchase.

You've never mentioned a standing desk before, Amber said.

I have! I said. I used to have one. I loved it! I said.

We'd kept shopping, filling a cart with $300 worth of groceries, which seemed to be what we always spent at

Costco, no matter how much or how little we put in the cart. It was also how much we would have spent if our cart had the adjustable height desk and nothing else.

On our way out, we stopped and each got a hot dog and a pop, and we shared a giant slice of pizza, which altogether was the cheapest meal we ever ate. I didn't say it out loud, but I made a deal with myself that the adjustable height desk would be my next reward. Reward for what was TBD.

I looked at the adjustable height desk in my temporary summer office in our temporary Tacoma home and my brain sparkled with the vision of all the words I was going to write there. Which was my goal for the summer. To write.

More specifically, my goal was to write a novel. *More* specifically—and, specifically, more ambitiously—my goal was to write a Great American Novel (GAN).

I hadn't told Amber. I hadn't said it out loud at all, and even when I thought it, I did so with a vague haziness that tried to blur specificity. Because it sounded silly, and because I didn't even really believe in the idea of a Great American Novel (GAN), and maybe most of all because I didn't want to make it real. I didn't want to jinx it.

We kept self-guided touring the house.

There was the kitchen; two bathrooms; a spare bedroom we'd probably never use for anything; a couple walk-in closets; another office that Amber probably wouldn't use but was there if she ever needed or wanted to; a laundry room; a loft we'd also probably never use, but I'd never had a loft before and I liked the idea and the sound of it, *loft*; a study with a big, comfy chair like for reading in, and three walls of built-in bookshelves, two of which were filled with books but the third was full of records, and in the corner was a stereo and record player, and so as much as I liked the idea of having a *study*, I thought of it as the "music-listening-room"; and one locked door that, because it was locked, we had no idea what was on the other side.

Ted and Alice are Harry Potter adults! I said, when we returned to the main room.

What? Amber said.

That sign on the locked door, I said. *No hoggles* allowed.

I saw the sign, Amber said. I didn't know that was a Harry Potter thing.

Neither of us had read any of the books or seen any of the movies, and I didn't really know what a hoggle was, but I was a human in the world, I knew it was a Harry Potter thing. I was surprised Amber didn't know.

Amber was gone and then she was back, bringing the sign back with her. *Muggles,* she said. She laughed her laugh like she was audibly rolling her eyes at me, and also telling me *I told you so,* and also pointing out what a dork I was, and also that she loved me.

Right, I said.

You kept saying 'hoggles,' Amber said.

Right, right, I said. Hoggle is the guy in *Labyrinth*. Muggles are… I don't know what they are, but I know they're a Harry Potter thing, I said.

If you say so, Amber said.

She put the sign down on the TV stand and we walked outside, out onto a giant wraparound deck. It looked out at that same view as the house's main room with the wall of windows of the Puget Sound and the islands and land on the other side and the Olympic Mountains above it all. We walked to where it wrapped around to the other side of the house, and that view looked out at Mount Rainier.

The mountain is out! I said.

Amber smiled because she loved that I loved the mountain and the water and the view and also because she loved the mountain and the water and the view too, and I smiled because her loving the mountain and the water and the view made me love it all even more.

Anything and everything felt possible. Maybe I *could* write a Great American Novel (GAN)! Or maybe a Great Washington Novel (GWN). A Great Pacific Northwest

Novel (GPNWN)? A Great Tacoma Novel (GTN)? Were there already any of those? I wasn't sure.

Any which way, I decided an adjustable height desk from Costco could be my reward for whatever I wrote here, Great or not, novel or something else, American or Washington or Pacific Northwest or Tacoma or otherwise.

We should do it out here on the deck with this beautiful view one night, Amber said.

We should, I said.

Not yet though, neither of us said, though we both knew it wasn't now yet.

We went inside and did it on the bed though. It was now for that, apparently.

After, we made cocktails and sat in chairs in front of the giant wall of windows and spent our first night in our temporary summer house staring out at our temporary summer view.

We should go on a walk tomorrow, Amber said.

OK! I said.

Get out and explore our temporary summer neighborhood! Amber said.

I got up and made us another round of cocktails and we watched as God tucked the sun in for sleep and opened up the sky behind the Olympics, showing off never-before-seen pinks and blues and purples and oranges hidden inside the universe until this very moment of birth.

We walked a few flat blocks and turned west into a hill that went all the way down to the waterfront. A giant hill, a crazy steep incline, a forever walk. It went like this: down down down down down down flat-for-a-block down down down down flat-for-a-block down down down down down down down, etc.

We passed a few people going the other direction, up, in full mountain climbing gear, and we passed a few other people who cheered us on and told us what champions we were, and also how beautiful we were, and also how they could tell, just by looking at us, that we were smart and kind and big-hearted and probably funnier than anyone they'd ever met.

At the bottom, we looked back up from where we came and saw our temporary summer house at the summit of the mountain.

We walked along the waterfront, pointing out to each other seals in the water and the Olympics out beyond the water and Rainier behind us, and then we turned around and walked back the way we'd come, pointing out differ-ent seals in the water or maybe the same seals in different places and the Olympics out beyond the water and Rainier now out ahead of us. We marveled at all the beauty and shared our disbelief that this temporary summer opportunity had dropped into our laps. Nothing had ever dropped into our laps before. Or, if something had, we'd forgotten. And if we'd forgotten, it didn't count.

We returned to the bottom of the giant hill that would return us to our temporary summer home.

I don't want to, Amber said.

We have to, I said.

I know, Amber said. But I don't want to.

We started walking and it went up up up up up flat-for-a-block up up up up flat-for-a-block up up up up up up up, etc.

That was beautiful, Amber said, when we were finally back atop the hill.

It really was, I said.

I don't want to ever do it again though, Amber said.

OK, I said. We don't have to.

We should do this every day though, Amber said. A walk of some kind.

OK, I said.

Almost every day anyway, Amber said. We'll probably be busy some days.

Sure, I said.

And thereafter we did. We never walked up or down that hill together again, but every day we went on a walk around our neighborhood, or we drove down to the waterfront and walked along that, or we drove to another neighborhood and walked around that. Almost every day anyway. We did end up busy some days.

ONE OF THE DAYS WE DIDN'T GO ON A WALK

We went and visited my parents. They lived a couple exits down the freeway from where I'd grown up. They'd moved the year after I'd moved away, and so the house was one I'd never lived in, in a neighborhood I'd never called home, but the house was full of all the same stuff that had filled the house I'd grown up in, and the neighborhood was close enough, and so similar, that it seemed almost like a lie to say it wasn't home. It was all familiar and not, comfortable and not, recognizable and not. It was all just askew enough to become something of an uncanny valley version of home.

My dad barbecued ribs and my mom made sides and we ate around the dinner table I'd grown up eating at. My dad told Amber the story of the time he threw me in the lake and my mom got out our photo albums and Amber laughed and smiled and asked follow-up questions and glowed and made it all feel even more like home.

Hours and hours disappeared like that was what they were made to do, and it was dark out and we said we should be getting home, but then on our way home we stopped at my best friend's place and had a couple of cocktails with him and his wife.

Versions of this would keep happening for the rest of the summer, but that Tacoma—the Tacoma of my family and my friends and a metaphorical magic of childhood and memories and nostalgia—and this Tacoma—the temporary summer Tacoma of fantasy houses with mysterious locked doors and fictional versions of friends coming to visit and a possible literal magic of changing landscapes and wormholes and time travel—are different, and this story is really about the latter, and so this is the only time I am going to tell you about the former.

By the time we finally got home, it was time for bed.

I woke up at sunrise. I never woke up at sunrise, but I never woke up in this place, in this time zone, in this body, in this everything.

West Coast Aaron felt younger and more confident, was more of a morning person, more handsome and capable, stronger, capable of lifting heavier weights and running farther and faster than he ever had before, and lots of other mores and biggers and betters too.

So I woke up at sunrise, my body clock still catching up and the non-clock parts of my body outpacing me. I was meeting myself somewhere in the middle.

I drove down the giant hill, parked, ran along the waterfront. Two miles in, it felt better than any run I did at home, and by mile four, it didn't even feel like I was running.

When I got back, Amber was awake and working, by which I mean her laptop was open and she was watching *Boy Meets World*.

How was your run? Amber said.

The Puget Sound picked me up like a baby and showed me a glimpse of heaven, I said.

OK, Amber said. Did you put on sunscreen?

I forgot, I said.

Amber made an angry face and tsk'ed me like I was in trouble.

I showered and then went into my temporary summer office. I lowered the adjustable height desk all the way and sat and opened my laptop, ready to work. Ready to write. Ready for day one, page one of my Great American Novel (GAN).

I stared at the blank Google doc on my laptop. At home, I used Word, but here I'd decided to use Google docs. I don't know why.

I looked up out the window at my idyllic view of the water and the islands out in it and the mountains out past the horizon line and then I looked down at the blank screen and back up at the view, back and forth and forth and back and back and back and back and back and forth and forth and forth and back…

You wanna go on a walk? Amber said from the other room.

I reeled myself back into my body, my body back into the room.

I wondered what time it was. It didn't matter. Amber was either clocking out early, or was going to take a break in the middle of her workday, or hours had passed with me watching the movie of the Puget Sound.

Giving myself allowance and encouragement and permission, and freeing myself from labels and definition and the locked rooms of expectation and preconception, and leaving room for and being open to inspiration and change and letting things become whatever they wanted, all seemed to be at odds with keeping track of hours and minutes. West Coast Aaron was free from the Tyranny of Time.

Sure! I said back to Amber.

I looked back at my screen and was startled to find it still empty. Buzzing all through my muscles and veins was the feeling of having been productive for anywhere from half an hour to three full days.

Just let me finish this real quick, I said.

I put my fingers on the keys and told them to write something.

I looked up out my window and out at the view and typed.

I looked back at my screen and it said, *The Puget Sound picked me up like a baby and showed me a glimpse of heaven.*

It was OK. It could probably be better, and I knew I could fall into the trap of overusing heaven as a metaphor or image or whatever if I wasn't careful, but it felt good, it felt *right*, and that was something. Sometimes that is everything.

Going on runs back home, in my normal life, I mostly listened to podcasts or audiobooks. I liked the conversations, the narratives. The parasocial relationships.

In Tacoma, I only ever listened to music. I wanted to dance instead of run, I wanted a soundtrack.

I discovered a handful of albums I'd never listened to by artists I'd listened to all the time. TV on the Radio's *Seeds*. The National's *Sleep Well Beast*. Cave In's *Heavy Pendulum*.

I don't know why hadn't even realized they'd been released.

I'd listen to these albums and run my way back to being 36 or 39 or 44, the ages I'd been when I'd not listened to them when they were released.

Every run a time machine to a younger self I'd never been.

A Different Tacoma

Everything seems different, I said.

What do you mean? Amber said.

We were walking through our temporary summer neighborhood and it felt different than it did the day before.
Which was part of what I meant, but not all of it.

I don't know exactly, I said. Just… different.

As if wanting to help me prove my point, we walked past
a house with a full-size basketball court in their yard, complete with overhead lights that I imagined they could turn
on in the evenings and play in the dark when they wanted.

I don't think that basketball court was there yesterday, I
said.

Amber looked at it, considered. Yeah, I don't remember it
either, Amber said. But probably we were just talking and
distracted.

Sure, I said. Maybe. But that's just one example. It's everything. Everything feels just a little different. Different
from yesterday, but different from when I was little too.

I think that's just called growing up, Amber said.

Sure, I said again.

We kept walking and I realized there weren't any speed bumps in the road. I was pretty sure there'd been speed-bumps yesterday.

Or maybe it's called nostalgia, Amber said.

I thought about everywhere we'd been the previous few days. How everything had looked like the town I'd grown up in and also like somewhere I'd never been before. Somewhere that had maybe never even existed before we'd shown up.

Or maybe it's just called life, Amber said.

I stopped in the middle of the road and looked behind us, then back out ahead. I looked out across Puget Sound that went off to the edge of the earth. I looked up into the universe of possibility above us.

I looked at Amber and smiled. Sure, I said one more time. That's probably it.

MOUNTAINS LIKE WHITE KNIVES

I woke up sometime during the imaginary hours between sunrise and Amber's alarm. I drove down to the water, parked, ran along the waterfront. That crisp ocean air curlicued off the water and washed a clean, crisp fountain of youth over me. I ran even farther and faster than the day before. I felt even better and more awake and more alive and more human than ever before. It felt like a kind of baptism. Maybe it was.

I got home and Amber was working, by which I mean her computer was open and she'd gone back to sleep. I took a shower and went to the office and opened my laptop, ready to write.

The Puget Sound picked me up like a baby and showed me a glimpse of heaven.

I laughed at myself, and then wanted to delete it, but 16 words were more than 0.

I went and got my phone. My buddy, Kevin, had texted me and our other buddy, D.T., that he was feeling a surge of hope and healing coming his way.

D.T. texted that he was thinking of applying to a job, that he was hitting the point where he hated what he does.

I texted them that I went on a run along the waterfront the day before and again that morning, and that the view was like a painting, and the run had made me feel like a teenager, and the air had baptized me and now I was born anew as West Coast Aaron.

D.T. texted that he needed a fucking break from… life.

Kevin texted back that life doesn't allow breaks for artists.

I texted that I was currently taking a break from life, and that I recommend it.

I transcribed D.T.'s and Kevin's texts into a Google doc file and then kept typing and typing and typing and typing and typing, thinking about ideas and situations and words and phrases and sentences that made myself laugh and that I imagined and hoped would make D.T. and Kevin laugh too. I wrote them all down, one after another after another after another, while Amber sat on the couch and watched *Boy Meets World* and replied to emails and sometimes moved imaginary money around in amounts greater than we'd ever see in our lives.

My screen started swirling and it reached out and grabbed me and pulled me in. I fell down a long deep dark tunnel, landing somewhere that looked and felt familiar. It reminded me of this place, that when the writing was going well, felt like what I'd heard and read athletes describe as The Zone. I watched an odd, fun Richard Linklater-like version of a movie of my last few days, and the movie ended and the credits rolled and the houselights came back on and I was sitting at my desk in front of my computer, staring at all these sentences and paragraphs and scenes and pages full of text.

I read over the story that had manifested on my screen and couldn't tell if it was good. It was fun, it made me laugh out loud a couple of times, but also there was a scene that grabbed my heart and twisted and squeezed in this way that hurt so good, and it had a pretty great ending, real sur-prising-yet-inevitable shit that recontextualized the whole and made me want to go right back to the beginning and reread it all again, and also it made me think a little new and differently about myself and life and the world.

I looked up and out at my view. In the distance, the mountains were beautiful and jagged, cutting across the horizon like a saw. I thought of that Hemingway story, and even though nothing about my story felt similar to that one—it wasn't almost all dialogue, it wasn't about a couple, there wasn't an abortion talked around but un-spoken and driving the story, it wasn't set in Europe, it wasn't really Hemingwayesque in any way—or maybe not *even though* but *because* it wasn't any of those things, I thought it would be funny to reference and echo its title, and so I thought about how I might be able to do that, and I thought and thought and typed one out, but didn't really like it, and then thought and thought and thought and thought some more, and finally landed on something that felt like it worked well enough, so I added that title and then I sent the file to D.T. and Kevin, saying they didn't have to read it, but I just wrote this new story, and it wasn't really *about* them, but they appeared in it.

Do you want to go on a walk? Amber said.

I closed my laptop and put on my shoes, and we went on another similar but different walk than the day before.

Life felt lighter. Brighter. Bigger with possibility.

I went on a run almost every morning, and every afternoon or evening Amber and I went on a walk together.

They were exercise, and they were a way of enjoying the weather, and they were meditative, and they became a way of discovering and seeing and learning what was around us.

Walks! I recommend them.

We walked up and down our block, neighboring blocks. Around and around and around the neighborhood.

When I was little—10 or 11, maybe 12—one of my friends, Matty, had all these pieces of paper taped up on his wall with maps he and his dad had drawn of whatever video game they were trying to beat. *Legend of Zelda*, for a while. *Metroid*. Other games I don't remember the names of. I'll never forget those maps though.

I remembered and thought of those maps and started drawing this temporary town of ours, after every walk.

They were record-keeping, and they were a way of making my life a little more organized, and they often acted as a kind of diary, and they became a way of even more deeply discovering and seeing and learning what was around us.

One day, walking along the waterfront, we saw a seal in the water, so I added a seal to my map of the waterfront. Another day, I laid down in the grass and fell asleep in the sun, so I wrote a bunch of Zs in my drawing of the park. *Zzzz.*

I taped the map up to the wall behind my desk. Because that's what Matty had done, and because I liked the way it decorated the room. I stood at the adjustable height desk and wrote and looked up at the Puget Sound and behind me at my map of this town. I created worlds and gazed out at the magic of a created world and studied my rec- reation of that created world.

Everything became both smaller and larger than it was, both more real and more mystical, more tangible and im- possible to know.

It also all became how I kept started keeping track of how everything around us kept mysteriously changing.

I went on my morning run and got back and Amber was in bed, watching *Boy Meets World*.

How's work? I said.

Pretty good, she said. Kinda busy.

I gave her a kiss and then pulled back the sheets and raspberried her tummy and then her underwear looked at me and said to kiss them so I did.

Mmmm, Amber said.

I liked the sound of that, so I kissed her on her underwear again.

Mmmmmm, Amber said again.

I liked the sound of that even more that time so I laid down and kept kissing and Amber kept mmmm'ing. I heard a ding, and I looked up and she was twisted over a little, on her computer, probably replying to an email or moving money around or doing something with spreadsheets that I didn't understand.

I kissed her underwear again, and then again, and again, and then I moved them to the side and kept kissing her. She mmmmm'ed and I kissed and she mmmmm'ed and I kissed and she mmmmm'ed and I kissed. I went slower and faster and moved up and down and went faster and slower and moved left and right and she mmmmm'ed, and then finally she oh, oh, ohhh, Oh, ohhhhh, OHHHHHH'ed. I felt her slump, and I stopped kissing and laid down next to her.

I looked across her to see which it was, email or spreadsheets, but it was back to playing *Boy Meets World*. Only it was Fred Savage instead of Ben. Because it was *The Wonder Years* instead of *Boy Meets World*.

When did you start watching *The Wonder Years?* I asked.

I don't watch *The Wonder Years,* Amber said.

But, I said. I pointed at her laptop screen.

I gotta pee, Amber said.

She went to the bathroom, and I watched Kevin Arnold and Winnie Cooper and Paul Pfeiffer, and then Amber returned and it was Cory Matthews and Topanga and Shawn. I didn't know Topanga or Shawn's last names; they weren't etched into my brain forever next to the phone numbers of my childhood home and my grandmother and my best friend like Winnie's and Paul's.

How'd you do that? I said.

Do what? Amber said.

I don't know, I said. And I didn't. I often don't.

My buddy Kevin came to visit. Said it'd do him good to get out of Portland for a couple days—new scenery, change of pace, leave the normal life problems and complications and stresses behind. We'd also been wanting to hang out while I was in Tacoma for the summer. The new scenery and change of pace and leaving behind of life's problems and complications and stresses were all bonuses.

The last week had been nothing but rain and gray and cold, but now it was sunny and blue skies and warm. It was beautiful. The kind of day that makes the rainy, gray, cold, hard, ugly, depressing ones worth it.

Amber and I made us all pizzas in the pizza oven we'd splurged on and bought for our temporary summer life. We walked downtown and got a couple beers.

The next day was even sunnier, bluer skies, warmer. Even impossibly, magically more beautiful. The kind of day that can make you forget life's problems and complications and stresses even exist.

We went out for happy hour at a restaurant on the waterfront, eating oysters and tuna tartar and beef skewers and pineapple shrimp, and drinking beers and cocktails and oyster shooters. We told stories and laughed at each other's stories. We took turns saying how beautiful the day was, how wonderful life could be, and agreeing when others said how beautiful the day was, how wonderful life could be.

Full and a little tipsy, we walked along the waterfront and Kevin said he really wanted to see an orca. Do you think we'll see an orca? Kevin said. How magical would it be if we see an orca? he said. I guess it isn't really orca season, is it? he said. I kinda feel like it would solve all my problems and complications and stresses if we get to see an orca, he said.

I couldn't remember if I'd ever seen an orca. It felt both like I had and hadn't. Impossible but likely.

I told Kevin we'd seen a few seals swimming around in the water and he asked if there were sea lions too. I said I thought there were, but I wasn't sure. I'm not actually sure I know the difference between a seal and sea lion, I said.

I guess I don't either, Kevin said.

We went out for more drinks and found a tiki bar. Inside, we were at an all-inclusive beach resort in a shipwrecked boat in an underground cave on an island. We sat in beach chairs by a water feature and became pirates and sailors and explorers and mermaids and mermen and sea captains and sea monsters. Waves crashed around us and a whale spouted water into the air and an octopus asked if we wanted another round. We ordered another round.

We shared more stories and we reshared the same stories we'd already shared earlier and we recapped the last couple of days and we smiled and laughed and were merry.

We cheersed orcas, and seals and sea lions, and waterfronts and tiki bars and friendship.

The walk and the day and our lives and the view and the sun on our faces and sharing stories and sharing meals and cheersing drinks and escaping our lives together for a couple of days and friendship—ours, specifically, but also just friendship in general—was magical.

We walked back home and didn't see any orcas or seal or sea lions. That was ok though.

Kevin returned home to Portland and Amber and I took a daytrip to the island we could see from our wall of windows.

The ferry ride was fun and exciting, everything shimmering and sparkling and bursting with beauty. The water like diamonds in the sunlight, the city bursting up out of the green blur of surrounding tress like a prehistoric forest giving birth to a science fiction city from the future.

We watched as the island we were headed to got closer, and we looked behind us and watched as the neighborhood we were living in for the summer got farther away. Amber pointed toward our temporary summer home. I think it's that one! I said, pointing where Amber was pointing. I moved my arm and pointed at the shore a little farther south and said that was where I'd grown up. I pointed at the park where we'd hung out in high school, and at the parking lot where we'd skated, and at the place where a tragedy had happened that feels too sad and both too personal and also too not-my-story-to-tell to write down here.

On the island, we drove along the coast and commented on the tide being so low. We walked through a farmers market, we ate lunch and had a drink, we walked through the downtown like tourists to whom everything is new and discoverable and anything is possible. We drove across the island to a park where we went on a hike through the woods, and we walked along the beach. We saw a sign about local sea animals. The sign told us about the seals and sea lions and porpoises and orcas in these waters, on a scale of how frequently they can be seen, from common to occasional to seldom. There *are* sea lions here! I said. We told stories and laughed and smiled and retold stories from the previous few days and then we retold stories from the previous few hours and we laughed and smiled some more. We drove back across the island and got another drink and another meal and that's the promise of days like that. Of days like these. We drove along the coast going the other way and commented on the tide now being so high.

On the ferry ride home, we went to the top deck and watched the island recede behind us. The sun was starting to set, bouncing off the water. The whole of Tacoma around us lit up in glowing Vegas neon and gold.

There's a whale off the right of the ferry, a voice announced over a loudspeaker.

Everyone on the ferry ran to the right side of the boat, hoping to see.

Amber got there first. I saw it! she said. I saw the orca!

Everyone stared at the water, staring into the sun bouncing off the water, staring out into the future and the past and everything in-between, looking for a quick glimpse of something to prove that God believed in them as much as they did in Him.

I saw something in the water. It submerged, surfaced a little further away, then submerged again. A seal or sea lion, probably; a fin of a porpoise, possibly; an orca, I want to be able to say.

I kept watching and watching and watching and watching and watching but didn't see anything else.

I wondered if Amber saw the same thing I did, or something else. I wondered if she saw the orca and I missed it, or if she saw a seal or sea lion but wanted it to be a whale and so believed it was, or if I saw a whale but was too doubtful of the world and so believed it wasn't.

The same voice over the loudspeaker told us that we were almost to shore and to return to our vehicles. Our trip and our journey and our day almost over. I thought, for a moment, about how, before we knew it, our temporary summer life was going to already be over. But not yet.

I closed my eyes. I felt the sun on my face and the beginnings of the sunset air on my skin. I was silent and still and unthinking, and for a brief moment the world was complete and beautiful nothing.

I opened my eyes and saw an orca, and then another, and another, and another, and another. They were everywhere. Cresting, submerging, spraying water up through their blowholes, swimming all around us. I watched and I smiled and I laughed and I thought about how sometimes, every now and then, if you're paying attention, if you're open to it, the world can be more than you could ever imagine, even if only for the briefest of moments.

I closed my eyes and felt that sun wash over me again, and opened my eyes and the whales were gone. Just like that.

We returned below deck and got in our car and waited to be told when it was our turn to exit the ferry, back to the mainland. Back to our normal lives.

Magic Is Everywhere, Slowly, Slowly

The map grew, covering the wall behind my desk.

My walking became farther, longer, and also a little more methodical. I searched for new streets, alleys, trails, pockets of neighborhoods to add to my drawing. Every walk felt different, because every walk *was* a little different, but not only because of that.

One day, there'd be no indication a Little Free Library had ever existed where I'd taken a book from the day before. A swingset that had been on the west end of a park was now on the east side. I'd turn down a road I'd been down plenty before, but it would be all new.

Amber said I was likely confused. Misremembering.

You never remember anything, she said. Smiling, teasing.

I know, I know, I said, laughing back. Ha. Haha.

And what do you mean the west side of the park. You never know directions, Amber said.

I didn't say anything to that. It was true but also not. I didn't want to argue with her, and I didn't want to argue with reality.

But I wasn't confused, I hadn't just misremembered. I never had any idea which direction was which in the middle of the country, but here we had mountains, we had the Puget Sound.

And there was the Little Free Library, right there on my map. There was my little drawing of a swing, on the left side of my drawing of the park.

I found a trail leading into the forest between the waterfront and our temporary summer home. Only a few steps into the woods, I could already no longer see the city or the waterfront behind me. It was all and nothing but forest. The forest floor all leaves and twigs and ferns and moss.

I hiked and hiked and remembered hikes from when I was little, hikes through forests where I'd imagine Bigfoot always just beyond sight, and then I was already exiting, back into a neighborhood. The city. I hadn't realized I'd been climbing, hadn't noticed any incline at all, but I was back atop the hill, mere blocks away from our temporary summer home.

When I got home, I added a forest to my map. I drew a spiral at the entrance to the trail.

What's that? Amber said.

That's the wormhole, I said, the word for it appearing out of nowhere as I said it.

OK, Amber said.

On the forest on my map, I wrote, "Wormhole."

A Scene Recalling *Stand By Me*

I went on a run and returned exhausted. The sunniest, hottest day of the summer yet. I was seal-slick with sweat and sat down on the ground in the driveway, catching my breath and letting my body cool down, waiting to become myself again.

I sat there, resting and resting and resting and resting, and then I looked up, and at the end of the driveway was a deer, staring at me.

I stared at the deer and it stared at me and I stared at it and it me and I it, like that, for a long time. Our eyes stared so deep into one another's we saw each other's hearts beating—*bup-bup, bup-bup.*

Staring into and then through the deer's eyes, into and through its body, watching that heart expand and deflate, over and over, I felt my own heart expand and deflate inside me. I felt the warmth of that process pump and glow and radiate through my whole body, and every time it expanded, it grew a little larger than it had before, and every time it deflated it shrunk a little less, so with every beat it grew and grew and grew and grew, until it was the size of my entire body. I was skin and bones and heart and nothing else.

I don't want to say it was romantic, but it wasn't not.

Ok, I'll say it. It was.

The deer looked at me and said, You're a fan of *Stand By Me*, aren't you?

I said I was. And then I asked how it knew.

You've included it in almost everything you've ever written, the deer said.

You've read my writing? I said.

Even sometimes when it really seems to have nothing at all to do with the larger narrative, the deer said.

OK, OK, I said. I was feeling honored and proud of myself that this deer had not just read me but maybe, seemingly, everything I'd written? But also it seemed to be using that to roast me, which felt weird.

The scene where Gordie sees the deer is one of your favorites, isn't it?

I said it was.

The deer reminded me that, in both the novella and the movie, Gordie says he considered telling his friends about the moment, but he didn't. He never told anyone until the moment of telling in the novella/movie.

I said I didn't need reminding of that.

I'm not sure why, but that's probably my favorite thing about that scene, I said.

That's exactly why it's so good and memorable, the deer said.

I smiled, proud like I'd gotten the right answer, even though it hadn't been a test. Or maybe it had.

The deer walked away and I went inside and told Amber the run felt great, but I was exhausted, and then I took a shower.

And I never told her, nor anyone else, about the deer, until now. I'm pretty sure I'm allowed. In fact, I think I'm *supposed* to tell you now. As part of this story.

It was a beautiful moment. One that felt good to have kept to myself, like a secret, but that feels a different kind of good to share with you now.

Fun and Stupid and Inventive All the Way Down

I kept writing new stories, copying and pasting things Kevin or D.T. texted to our groupchat into a Google doc and using it as a springboard into another 600-1800 word piece of silly, fun, exaggerated autofiction about us and writing and friendship and telling stories and life and seeing art and magic and beauty everywhere you look. Each time, I set out to write something fun and stupid and inventive but each just ended up being earnest and nostalgic and open-hearted.

But that's fun and stupid and inventive too, Kevin texted.

That's just your version, Kevin texted.

I wrote the bonkers version and yours is just a little happier and like you had a good day, Kevin texted.

D.T. didn't say anything. It was probably his kid's birthday or he was sick, or lifting kettlebells in his garage, or sick of me copying and pasting his texts and using them for stories or he was too sad from Kevin's last story that described heartbreak as like God sawing off parts of your body.

I wrote a story that included a long sentence listing reasons why maybe D.T. hadn't said anything in our groupchat, and that gave me an idea, so I paused writing that story and opened up another Google doc. I started a new, different story where God tells a woman to saw off her partner's limbs. It referenced the story of God telling Abraham to sacrifice his son, Isaac, only God didn't tell the woman in the story to sacrifice her partner, only to saw off his limbs. Also, God didn't stop her at the last minute like He did with Abraham. He let her go through with it. I kept writing, following every dumb and preposterous "what if?" It felt exciting. It was the most fun and stupid and inventive story I'd written yet. I sent it to Kevin and D.T.

I love it! D.T. texted.

Me too! Kevin texted.

I didn't even go that long without replying though, D.T. texted. You two dumb motherfuckers are out of control and need to get lives, D.T. texted.

I'm taking a break from my life! I texted.

Me too! Kevin texted. I mean, I'm either taking a break from my life or building a whole new one or shedding my last one like a snakeskin, or God sawed off all the appendages of my old life and I'm going to go on a drug journey through the desert and find all new appendages, or lives aren't real and none of this even matters.

That's fair, D.T. texted.

I really think this one was your most earnest and nostalgic and open-hearted story yet, Kevin texted.

Dammit.

I read back over the story and was shocked to discover he was right.

Also, I'd thought the story was all about a couple, using surreal body horror as a kind of echo for how you have to make sacrifices in a relationship, and that was all there, but also it was Kevin, not God, who told the woman maybe she should saw off her partner's limbs and then, later in the story, after a bunch of pages of the couple driving around and seeing the country together—Mt. Rushmore and the Badlands and Falling Water and Knott's Berry Farm and this one bar outside of Reno that early in their relationship they'd together read a short story about and Devils Tower and the Corn Palace and that baseball field in Iowa where they filmed *Field of Dreams*—all while she carried his limbless body around in a kind of babybjorn, and one day, shopping for snacks at a gas station, they run into their old friend, D.T., and he said she should saw off her own appendages too, and she did, and then, through the magic of love and sacrifice and speculative fiction, their limbs grew back, and with them, their hearts and their love for each other grew stronger too.

It was a little cheesy, I fear, but also had some of the best sentences I'd ever written. I reminded myself that sometimes those sentences only happen when you allow a little cheese.

I told Amber about the story. I described it and told her how I sent it to Kevin and D.T. and they said it was earnest and nostalgic and open-hearted, and how that surprised me, and also how when I reread back over it, I was surprised that they were in it at all. I told her about how writing is weird, how you'll have one idea and start writing it, but then it will become something else without you even meaning it to, sometimes without you even realizing it, and she looked at me like I was stupid. I'd told her some version of that a million times.

I expected her to make fun of me for writing story after story after story after story where Kevin and D.T. keep popping up, but instead she glommed onto the surreal body horror part. Which surprised me, because normally she looked at me like *what the fuck are you talking about?* when I described one of my more surreal or speculative stories, but also because I'd forgotten that was even what the story was about. I'd gotten so distracted by Kevin's and D.T.'s appearances in it.

Amber said she used to have this idea for a story about someone cutting off their skin so it would grow back healthier and blemish free.

I could write that story! I said.

I went into my temporary summer office and stood at my adjustable height desk and opened up a blank Google doc and started typing. I didn't think about what might make it a good story and I didn't ever stop to think about what should happen next, I just typed and typed and typed and typed and typed and typed.

In the story, the narrator cut off his skin so it would grow back healthier and blemish free. He worked from home and ordered delivery and never left the house, waiting and waiting and waiting and waiting and waiting to reenter the world as a whole new version of himself. But his skin never grew back. He didn't know what to do. He didn't know what to make of this miscalculation. Didn't have any idea how to make sense of this world at all, now that he thought about it. Then he had an idea. He sat down and wrote a story, and when he got stuck, these two characters, his friends, Devin and K.T., appear out of nowhere and tell him what to do next, or they do something funny or say some non sequitur that doesn't literally tell him what to do next and isn't technically funny but makes him laugh and gives him an idea for how to proceed. He finishes the story and sends it to the Devin and K.T. in his story.

Is this your whole thing now? D.T. texted.

I like it, Kevin texted.

I didn't say I didn't like it, D.T. texted.

I like it too, I texted. These are fun. Are they just dumb and repetitive though? I texted.

They feel like iterations, but not really repetitive, Kevin texted.

And so what if they are repetitive, D.T. texted.

The *so what* and also the word *iterations* gave me an idea, and I hurried back to my desk and wrote a story about a guy writing a story about a guy writing a story about a guy writing a story. I lost track of how many levels or layers of story-within-a-story it was.

I finished the story and sent it to Kevin and D.T., and they told me they liked it. Most of their favorite moments were what the third or fourth or ninth degree fictional versions of themselves said or did. It was possible they kept liking all these stories because they appeared in them. I had the idea of writing a Great American Novel, maybe the Greatest American Novel, where everyone alive made an appearance. It would be the first book ever that everyone alive read and liked.

Instead of working on a novel—a GAN or GWN or GPNWN or GTN or otherwise—I kept writing these dumb, fun stories. I didn't know what to do with them. They felt too meta for anyone else to care, but they were fun and Kevin and D.T. said they were fun, and when I told Amber I finished another and described it to her, she'd roll her eyes and look at me like *you're so dumb* or like *what the fuck are you talking about?* but also she said it sounded fun and she'd laugh and it would light up her face and the room and our lives and the world and God would smile down on us and say, Aaron, that one was even more fun and stupid and inventive than your last, and also even more earnest and nostalgic and open-hearted, and I kept writing stories like that, iterations of the same thing over and over and over and over and over and over and over.

How do we beat this? Amber said.

I was just back from a run and Amber was standing in my office, staring at my map on the wall. She hadn't really given it much attention or seemed to care about it at all. It was some weird thing I was doing on my own that she teased me about as being dumb, exactly because having fun and doing weird dumb things is what life it all about.

How do we beat this? Amber said again. What's our quest here? What's our primary objective of all this, do you think? Amber said.

Oh yeah. That reminds me—

SOMETHING I FORGOT TO TELL YOU

I don't remember if it was at the tiki bar or the oyster happy hour or when we made pizzas or what, but when Kevin was in town, we'd had a conversation about our Summer of Make-Believe. I'd kept calling it our temporary summer life, but he'd started calling it our Summer of Make-Believe.

Do you guys have any goals or anything for this Summer of Make-Believe, Kevin had asked.

Ess Em Bee, I said.

What? Kevin said.

Ess Em Bee, I said, and, Summer of Make-Believe, Amber said, both of us at the same time.

I looked at her and smiled.

He acronyms everything, Amber said. It's super dumb.

You love it, I said.

I do, Amber said.

I forgot Kevin was there and I leaned in toward Amber. We kissed and then we started to make out. We never did that in public. Maybe it was the oysters.

Wow, Amber said.

I wasn't sure if it was about the kiss or that it had happened at all or what.

Anyway, Kevin said. Anything on your summer bucket list or any goals or anything?

Amber looked at me and I looked at her and she looked at me.

Not really? we both said.

I thought about my goal of writing a novel, but I didn't want to say that out loud because I didn't want to jinx it and also because I didn't want to make it real and also because I still hadn't even started it. I'd just kept writing stories that were iterations of the same story, over and over and over.

You guys should come up with something! A list or a BINGO card or a primary objective or something, Kevin said.

A primary objective? I said.

I was surprised at the phrase and even more surprised to hear it from Kevin. He was normally telling me how everything isn't real and nothing matters and about these Buddhist principles of enlightenment.

A primary objective can act as a north star on your path toward enlightenment, Kevin said.

I wondered if I'd said out loud what I'd thought I'd only thought.

You didn't say it out loud, Kevin said. I'm just really enlightened.

I think our primary objective is just to have fun, I said. To enjoy ourselves and make the most of it.

Sure, sure, Kevin said. But that's too abstract. What you need is a *quest*.

Do we have to? Amber asked.

You don't *have* to do anything, Kevin said. That's the whole thing about life. Money and jobs aren't real. Quests and primary objectives and goals aren't real, Kevin said.

There was the Kevin I knew.

They aren't *real*, Kevin said again, but they can make things more fun.

Fun is real, I said.

Fuck yeah, it is, Kevin said.

What should our quest be then? I said.

That's up to you, Kevin said.

57

I think it was about then the waiter came by and asked if we wanted another round. Whether it was the waiter at the tiki bar or oyster happy hour though, I can't remember.

OK.

How do we beat this, what's our quest, what's our primary objective? Amber said, both of us staring at my map on the wall.

It looks like you're mapping out this city like a game you're trying to beat, Amber said. Like that Mikey kid you were friends with when you were little.

Matty, I said.

Right, Amber said. Matty.

I told you about that? I said.

Like a hundred times, Amber said.

I wasn't sure if I was more surprised that I'd told her and forgotten, or that I'd repeated myself so many times, or that she'd been listening any of those times.

I looked at my map on the wall. I thought of Matty and him explaining that he and his dad drew the maps because they kept getting lost and forgetting where they'd already explored and replaying the same loop over and over. I guess it did look like I was trying to beat Tacoma.

I guess it does look like that, I said.

Was that what I was doing? Was that why I'd started doing this in the first place?

Amber took a couple of steps forward and pointed at an empty space on the lower left just beyond where we'd so far explored and thus just outside of what I had so far drawn.

What's down here? Amber said.

I don't know, I said. We haven't gone down there yet.

And you don't know what's over there? Amber said.

I looked closer. I was looking at the map like a log of where I'd so far run and walked. I was looking at it not quite like something I'd invented, but almost. I'd forgotten what it actually was. A map. I knew the basics of this city. I knew it as well as anyone knows the city where they grew up and memorized as a child but then moved away and learned other cities for twenty years. I knew it like a ghost that my hand passed right through when I tried to reach out and touch it.

Oh yeah, I said. The mall is over down there.

A nostalgia storm rained down on me, washing me away in a time traveling river through being eight and ten and twelve and thirteen and fourteen and sixteen, going to the mall with my parents and with just my dad and with just my mom and with friends and by myself. It felt like scuba diving through a garden maintained by a beautiful, loving guardian angel, but also like drowning.

Amber put her mouth on mine and resuscitated me.

The room and my life and the world lit up in sunlight and warmth.

I forgot how good it feels to die and be brought back to life, I said.

Let's go to the mall tomorrow, Amber said.

Sure, I said.

THE MALL

The mall of my youth. The mall I went to and hung out at as a teenager, the mall my mom took me to for back-to-school shopping at the end of summer, the mall I think about and picture as the definition and prototypical example of a *mall*.

Almost every store was different, but also everything looked exactly the same. A copy of a copy. The Mall of Theseus.

One part nostalgia, one part time machine. One part panic attack, because shopping always gives me a bit of a panic attack; one part panic attack, because teleporting through time always gives everyone a bit of a panic attack. I assume. How could it not. Defying the laws of time and space and all that.

That Macy's used to be Bon Marche, I said.

OK, Amber said.

And that Nordstrom used to be Frederick & Nelson, I said.

OK, Amber said again.

I looked at Amber but she wasn't looking back at me and I wondered if it was because she didn't grow up with Bon Marche and Frederick & Nelson and so those stores didn't mean anything to her, or because she was just paying attention to which stores she wanted to go in and wasn't living inside the body and looking out through the eyes and thinking via the firing synapses of the brain of her childhood self.

Amber kept walking forward and I followed, though distracted. It was all a dream inside a memory inside a fog of deja vu.

Or maybe the Nordstrom used to be Mervyn's? I said.

It was hard to remember. Every single memory from my childhood was right there, right in front of me, each just beyond my grasp. Mall as photo album of my youth, only I'd been instructed I was forbidden to touch.

Amber pointed at a store I'd never heard of but also I was pretty sure was the same store that had always been there.

I'm going to try on some jeans, she said.

I told her I was just going to wander and feel nostalgic.

Of course you are, she said.

I got an Orange Julius and it tasted different than I remembered but also like I would give my life for a cute girl to notice me. I got a Cinnabon and it tasted basically the same as I remembered and also like my dad being proud of me for another perfect report card.

I went into the Apple Store that used to be KayBee Toys, and I flipped through cordless mice and headphones and phone cases thinking about *Star Wars* and *GI Joe* and *M.A.S.K.* action figures until an employee came over and asked if they could help me find anything.

No thank you, I said, and left.

I went into Spencer Gifts and it looked nothing like it used to when I was little, but it made me feel exactly like it used to when I was little. When the front of the store was all gag gifts but the back was like a softcore version of an adult toy store. I wasn't allowed back there.

I went to the back of the store and it felt risque and exciting and a little dangerous. It felt even more like being a kid than anything before it.

In the back back back of the store, there was a rack of clearance t-shirts. I flipped through them but then felt something odd, and then, behind the shirts, noticed something odd. There was a small rectangle of wall that didn't look like a door, but I somehow knew was one. I thought of Matty, and his maps, and playing video games with him. Him showing me these secret doorways and paths that you only knew were there if you knew they were there.

I got down on my hands and knees and opened the door and it opened to a tunnel. I crawled inside and closed the door behind me, and I crawled and crawled and crawled and crawled and finally found another door at the other end. It opened up into my childhood bedroom.

It was smaller than any bedroom I'd had since, but inside it again, it felt as big as the world. The walls were covered with posters of Bo Jackson and the Bash Brothers and Preki. There were two small bookshelves full of Hardy Boys books and Choose Your Own Adventure paperbacks, and on the bottom shelves were stacks of *Beckett Baseball Card Monthly.* Everything was neat and tidy, so organized, the way I'd always kept my room when I was little, before puberty and I stopped caring and it was always a mess.

I went to my closet and in the full body mirror hanging on its door, I saw my 11-year-old self looking back at me.

I was so tired.

I got in my bed, crawled inside my baseball sheets and curled up and fell asleep. I slept for a lifetime. In the morning, my parents woke me up; my dad said he made pancakes and my mom said to hurry up, it was her turn for carpool.

I woke up and stretched, same as I had every morning in this bed growing up. On my nightstand was a single key, which I didn't remember being there any morning growing up. I put it in my pocket and went out to the kitchen.

I ate pancakes and then I went back to my bedroom to get dressed but instead found the secret door that either hadn't been there when I'd been little or I hadn't yet had enough life experience to notice, and I crawled and crawled and crawled and crawled until I found the door at the other end, and then I was back in Spencer Gifts.

Those are all on clearance so you can't return them, a voice said.

I turned and looked and saw a young Spencer Gifts employee staring at me.

I looked at the sign on the rack of t-shirts that said *Clearance – Final Sale – No Returns.*

OK, I said.

I flipped through the shirts on the rack. They were all black. A couple were of bands I'd never heard of but could tell were band shirts, but then most were the same Nirvana and Alice in Chains and Black Sabbath and Metallica and Nine Ince Nails shirts kids had worn when I'd been probably whatever age the kids who currently bought these shirts at Spencer Gifts were.

I exited back to the main thoroughfare of the mall and sat in a giant massage chair. I thought about how, when I was little, I'd beg my parents to give me money that I could feed into one of those chairs and get a massage and they always said it was a waste of money, and now that I was an adult, with my own money to do whatever I wanted with, I'd never feed it into a mall chair for a massage. It seemed like a waste of money.

You want to share a pretzel? Amber said.

I looked up and Amber was there, standing in front of me.

Sure, I said.

How was your little nostalgia tour? Amber said.

I loved when she used my dumb little phrases back at me.

The Door That Was Supposed to Remain Locked

I want to know what's behind the door, Amber said one day after work.

What? I said.

You know, Amber said. The door that's locked. To the room or hallway or whatever where we're not supposed to go.

I'd forgotten all about it.

I'd wanted to know too, for the first couple of days, and then that want flittered away and I'd taken the door and that it was locked for granted and just forgotten all about it.

They say no hoggles allowed, I said, thinking it would be funny.

Muggles, Amber said.

I wasn't sure how she could not know they were from Harry Potter but she remembered the word and I couldn't.

I remember everything, Amber said.

Whatever, I said, to the hoggles/muggles correction and to her reading my mind and to her remembering everything and just to everything.

Oh! I said. I reached into my pocket and pulled out the key from my childhood bedroom.

Where did you get that? Amber said.

I forget, I said.

You forget everything, Amber said.

I tried the key in the locked door and—aha! of course!—it fit and turned. It unlocked the door.

I had a moment of feeling like maybe we shouldn't actually be doing that, but only a small moment, and only a small feeling, because then I was already pushing open the door.

Inside the room was a giant pile of fireworks. Bottle rockets and mortars and fountains and more mortars and more bottle rockets and roman candles and more mortars and more more more more more more more of everything. More fireworks than I'd ever seen, all in a big giant pile.

Isn't that your handwriting? Amber said.

I'd been so overwhelmed by the pile itself, I hadn't even noticed any handwriting. But there it was. A big piece of paper that read, *For later.* And, indeed, it looked like my handwriting.

I don't know, I said. I guess? Kinda? Maybe?

That's definitely your handwriting, Amber said.

I didn't write it! I said.

I didn't say you did, Amber said. I just said it's your handwriting.

I didn't write it though! I said again. I wasn't sure why, but I was on the verge of crying. Right there on the verge, teetering. Like I was waiting for the smallest nudge to tip me over and I'd go falling falling falling into an abyss of tears. Everything felt like too much.

I backed out of the room and Amber followed, and I slammed the door shut, turned the key and locked it again.

It's weird is all, Amber said.

She was right. It was weird. But what do you do with weird?

D.T. Comes to Visit

D.T. was standing at the end of my normal waterfront run, waiting for me. Like I'd just run a race and he'd come out to cheer me on at the finish line.

What are you doing here? I said.

You and Kevin kept texting about all the fun you guys had and I got jealous, D.T. said.

We did have a lot of fun, I said.

Shut the fuck up about it already, D.T. said. It's our turn to have fun, he said.

That seemed like kind of an aggressive way to start, but whatever. I was excited for another visitor.

How'd you know where to find me? I said.

You run this waterfront every morning, D.T. said. You won't shut up about it. And also I rode an orca up and it dropped me off on the beach right down there, so this was super convenient.

Ummmmm, I said, confused. I looked down at the beach

and then looked out at the water. Ummmmmmmm, I said.

Don't overthink it, D.T. said. He looked at his watch. It's happy hour!

Was it happy hour? Had my normally hour-long run turned into hours and hours?

Don't look so confused like that, D.T. said. Time isn't real.

I wasn't sure if he was making fun of Kevin or earnestly saying it, or maybe we had all just started talking a little like each other.

Let's get some drinks! I'm on vacation! And you're apparently on some kind of endless vacation or whatever the fuck you're calling it, D.T. said.

Temporary break from life, I said.

Sure, D.T. said. Whatever.

We walked into one of the restaurants on the water and got a cocktail and then another, and then we walked next door to one of the other restaurants on the water and got a couple rounds there. Life expanded, got big with joy and possibility.

Life feels so big and like anything is possible! I said. I was drunker than I'd thought.

Anything IS possible! D.T. said.

We ordered another round, and then one more because he was on vacation and I was on a temporary break from life and life was big and anything was possible. We paid our tab, then outside realized we were too drunk to drive. We could walk, I said, but then remembered the giant hill, and I got a side ache and started sweating from exhaustion.

The Wormhole! I said, suddenly remembering. I was excited. And drunk.

What the fuck are you talking about? D.T. said.

Dude you rode an orca here, just go with it, I said.

D.T. shrugged and just went with it, and we walked to the trail entrance to the Wormhole.

The Wormhole

We started walking on the trail, toward the Wormhole. Or maybe the whole trail was the "Wormhole"? I wasn't sure.

It looked different than before. Greener. Or maybe less green? Like there were definitely more trees, packed in more densely, or maybe they were more spread out and the trail felt more open.

I wondered if maybe it wasn't going to be a wormhole anymore, or somehow even wormholier. Or maybe the same amount and that was just growing up, nostalgia, life.

When do we get to the Wormhole? D.T. said.

I think maybe we're in it? I said. I think maybe it's all wormhole?

This doesn't feel like a wormhole, D.T. said.

He was right, it didn't. But also, how did he know what a wormhole felt like?

As if abracadabra'd, a clearing opened up in the woods, and three pirates sat around the flat table of a tree stump.

Are they going to take us to the wormhole? D.T. said.

I wasn't sure why he was asking me instead of them.

Why are you asking him instead of us? one of the pirates said.

I laughed.

You're in the wormhole, one of the other pirates said.

It's all wormhole, the third pirate said.

I knew it!

Whatever, D.T. said. What happens now? D.T. said.

You have to stump us with a riddle and then we let you pass through the wormhole, the first pirate said.

Why are there pirates in the forest? D.T. said.

You guys weren't here last time, I said.

It would make more sense if you guys were, like, ogres or something, D.T. said. Or witches maybe.

Or ghosts! I said. Like, the ghosts of Wormholes Past and Present and Future or something.

No, D.T. said. That would be dumb. This isn't *A Christmas Carol.*

Why would ogres or witches or ghosts make more sense than pirates? all three pirates said.

They said it in unison and then they all got a similar look on their face. Part surprise, part frustration. Then they disappeared. Just like that.

You stumped them! I said.

Look, D.T. said. He pointed at the tree stump they'd been sitting around.

The tree *stump* and the *stumping* the pirates with the riddle felt a little too easy, or cheesy. A little too something.

Language isn't real, D.T. said.

Has Kevin said that, I said.

I don't know, D.T. said. That guy doesn't think anything is real.

I walked closer to the stump, and the top was a dark, empty hole, like one of those pipes in *Super Mario Bros.*

We both jumped up onto the stump and stood there for a second, then we bent our knees, starting to crouch down. The Mario teleporting sound effect rang through

the forest, and we fell down the hole, falling, falling, falling, falling, falling.

Finally, instead of hitting the bottom, I was standing at
the front door of my temporary summer home. I didn't
know where D.T. was. We've never talked about it since.

The day after D.T.'s visit, it rained. All day. It rained and rained and rained and rained and rained and rained.

I hadn't realized until it started raining, but it had barely rained since we'd gotten to Tacoma. A little at first, and then blue skies for Kevin's visit and nothing but blue skies since. Which was odd because Tacoma and Washington and the whole Pacific Northwest is basically known for raining all the time. That's kinda its thing.

The thing about Tacoma, though, is that it doesn't actually rain as much as its reputation. And in the summer, especially, it is sunny and beautiful more often than not. Most people who know that try to keep it a secret though. Sometimes you have to keep secrets about things and places to hold onto their magic.

And also, when it does rain, it almost never does so hard. It is a trickle, a mist. Barely even *rain*, really.

Which made it especially surprising when we woke up one morning and it was *pouring*. It felt unlike itself. It felt Biblical. It felt like God said, *Let there be rain,* and no one had previously witnessed rain, or at least not like this, or at least had not given it name, and then the sky opened up, and then it opened a little more, and it kept ripping and tearing itself apart while all the water that had ever existed came tumbling down.

I sat in one of the chairs by the giant windows and watched, in awe.

An hour or a few days or a week passed. The water kept rising, spilling out over the waterfront, as water fell down from the heavens into this giant earthbound body of water, water raining down into water, water overflowing with water, water water water.

I had an idea. I went to my bag and got a magic erase marker and started transcribing the rain, translating the weather into story.

The sky lightninged and thundered, telling me the story was done, or maybe telling me I was at the climax and it was encouraging me to go bigger and weirder and more bombastic and more climactic, but I was pretty sure it was the former, so I wrote *THE END,* and then it stopped raining, just like that, and that was the end.

I stepped back, took it all in. I felt pretty proud of myself.

I took a photo and sent it to Kevin and D.T.

What the fuck is that, D.T. texted back.

I think this one is my new favorite yet! Kevin texted.

How did you even read that? D.T. texted.

I just opened up my mind's third eye and let the story wash over me and get inside me and live through me, Kevin texted.

Oh, is that all? D.T. texted.

I put my phone away and, now that it had finally stopped raining, I asked Amber if she wanted to go on a walk.

The Zoo

There is something about sharing a moment of wonder with someone you love. Being next to them. Being able to not just witness the moment with them but through their eyes.

That's what I was thinking, standing next to Amber in the aquarium, watching the jellyfish.

We'd been at the zoo an hour or two, but the elephant had stood so completely still the entire time we'd stared at it we could have just been looking at a statue, and the tiger area was closed because they'd had to euthanize it the week before, and the monkeys were all either hiding out of sight or in another enclosure. The day was feeling like a bust. We'd needed some wonder.

They aren't real, Amber said. Kept saying. They aren't real, they seem made up, this is make-believe, I don't think they're real, they can't be real, she said. Over and over and over and over.

I was sure we'd seen jellyfish together before, but maybe not. This moment of wonder and make-believe felt new. Sometimes life feels like a series of finding out I was wrong about something I was sure of. Other times, vice versa.

I've tried not being sure of anything, so I'd never be wrong, but somehow that only made me wrong more often.

We moved from one jellyfish display to the next. These ones weren't real and seemed made up and were make-believe and weren't real too, albeit in slightly different ways.

What even is their purpose? Amber said, as we moved on to one more next display.

What even is *our* purpose? I said, and laughed.

I bet if I did a bunch of mushrooms, I would know, Amber said. I waited for her to laugh but she didn't.

Instead, as if a genie in a bottle or Beetlejuice being summoned, my buddy Kevin appeared out of nowhere, suddenly right there in the aquarium with us.

Come with me, Kevin said, and led us over to a bench where we all sat. He didn't grab and hold our hands, but it felt like his aura did.

I remembered a dream I'd had the night before of being in a parking lot with Kevin and our other buddy D.T. and doing drugs that Kevin kept pulling out of his armpit. I wondered if this whole zoo and aquarium visit was a dream too. Maybe the elephant actually had been a statue. A dream elephant statue!

This isn't a dream, Kevin said.

I wondered if he could read my mind or if I'd said that aloud. Either way, it felt reassuring. That the zoo had had to euthanize a tiger was sad, but that was life. The reality of life sometimes being sad felt less depressing than my subconscious having dreamt such sadness.

Kevin reached into a fanny pack I hadn't realized he was wearing and pulled out a baggie and gave a handful of drugs to Amber and then another to me.

These are hero doses, Kevin said. You're going to experience ego death and feel at home in this world, maybe for the first time.

I just wanted to see and understand our purpose, Amber said.

That'll happen too, Kevin said. Probably. Same thing, basically, he said.

I'm not sure if I want to see God or not, I said.

You don't have to call it God, Kevin said.

I wasn't sure if that was reassuring or a riddle. I decided it didn't really matter.

Kevin ate his drugs and said something about being our guide through the cosmos or our drug warrior priest or our hippie spiritual professor or something like that. And then he said, actually, nevermind, and he took back the drugs he'd given us and ate those too.

Kevin looked deep into Amber's eyes and then deep into mine, and something about the way he looked at us, I could tell he could see all the way inside to our beating hearts. He could see us each for who we truly were. It made me a little uncomfortable, if I'm being honest, but it was beautiful too.

You were almost right, Kevin said.

What? Amber said.

Jellyfish aren't really real, Kevin said.

I knew it! Amber said.

But nothing else is real either, Kevin said.

This again, I thought. Or maybe I said it.

In fact, Kevin said. Jellyfish are so not real, that in this fucked up world of ours where nothing is real, they might be the only real thing that exists, Kevin said.

What? Amber said again.

Exactly, Kevin said.

And then, just like that, Kevin was gone, disappeared as suddenly and mysteriously as he'd appeared, and then someone over the aquarium loudspeaker announced that the zoo was closing and everyone needed to work their way toward the exits.

I was pretty sure the zoo was open until 5, at least, and maybe even 7 or 8 or 9, and we'd gotten there close to noon, and I really didn't think we'd been there longer than a couple hours. But time seemed to keep doing that lately.

I went on a run and listened to TV on the Radio's *Seeds*. Tunde Adebimpe sang,

> Oh, I keep telling myself
> "Don't worry, be happy"
> Oh, you keep telling yourself
> "Everything's gonna be okay"

The song got into my legs, bloomed up through my whole body, massaging my muscles while I ran, urging me into a gear and conditioning I didn't know I had. I was on summer vacation and had no worries, in general and specifically that anything wasn't going to be okay, but felt a wave wash over me that everything was going to be even okay-er.

I was already back at my car but my body wanted to keep going, so I told my phone to keep playing "Trouble" on repeat, and I ran along the waterfront in the other direc-tion this time, and then back again, the song and my brain and the Puget Sound alongside me and the mountain out ahead of me and the big open expanse of clear blue skies overhead, and a heaven of angels overhead that, all telling me, over and over and over and over and over and over about everything being okay and a world of happiness and comfort and joy and love.

After the run, the song still looping through my mind, I texted Kevin and D.T. Don't worry, be happy.

D.T. texted, Like that annoying dumbass song from the 80s?

I texted back, Actually, yeah, I guess. But I was quoting TV on the Radio not Bobby McFerrin. But maybe they were quoting Bobby McFerrin?

Kevin texted, Probably.

D.T. texted, Dumbass.

I texted back that everything was gonna be okay.

How was your run? Amber said, when I got home.

I told her it was good and that it gave me an idea, and I went into my temporary summer office and raised the desk to standing height and stood and I typed out my and Kevin's and D.T.'s texts and then I typed out the lyrics to TV on the Radio's "Trouble." I opened up YouTube and watched the music video for Bobby McFerrin's "Don't Worry Be Happy" and then I typed out the lyrics to that, and then watched the video again, then again and then again and a set of waves of joy crashed over me and the water parted, opening up into a portal to 1988. I swam through it and was 10 years old again, watching the video with my parents, and then an undercurrent grabbed me and pulled me under and then spit me back out and I washed ashore back in the present, standing at the desk and staring at my computer. I started typing. I typed and typed and typed and typed and typed.

You wanna go on a walk? Amber said.

Sure! I said. I can be ready here in a few. I just want to re-read back over what I wrote.

I read back over what I wrote, my heart growing warm and crinkly as I read an essay about Bobby McFerrin's "Don't Worry Be Happy" and my childhood and my parents and friends and family and being adopted and all the love and support and encouragement I'd been blessed with, and as I got to the end, it culminated in memories of my grand-mother and how much I missed her. She was the reason I'd ended up in Tacoma in the first place. We moved in large part to be closer to her. Growing up, we'd go to her house almost every week, and she'd make a big dinner and host, and we'd all watch TV together and I'd play in her giant backyard. Her house was bigger than ours, so when I was little, it had seemed big enough to hold the entire world. And that's how it felt when we were there. She passed away when I was in college, and then I graduated and moved away, and Tacoma stopped being my home even while al-ways being what I thought of as home.

I finished reading the essay I had no memory of writing and told Amber I was almost ready. I grabbed my phone to tell Kevin and D.T. I'd apparently written a new essay and saw I had a missed call and a voicemail.

My phone said it was from an unknown number.

I clicked the button to listen to it.

Hello, Aaron, my grandmother's voice said.

I started crying.

I just wanted you to know how proud I am of the grandson and man and writer and human you've become, my grandmother's voicemail said.

Are you OK? Amber said, hearing me sobbing from the other room.

Everything's gonna be okay, I said, not meaning to but singing it.

THE CITY KEPT GROWING WHILE THE
AMOUNT OF SUMMER LEFT WAS SHRINKING

Everyday I went on a run or a walk by myself or a walk
with Amber, and often some combination, and sometimes
all three.

I explored the city and came home and added to my map,
and every few walks, every few days, every now and then,
a new little pocket of magic would unveil itself for me to
discover.

I found a tree that, when climbed, took me all the way up
into the clouds, opening up into a view of the entire city.

I found a park bench that, when sat on, would often—
not *always*, but often—give me an idea and inspiration for
a new story.

I found a swingset in a different park that, when swinging,
placed me at whatever moment in my life I'd been thinking
about, allowing me to watch the memory and moment
play out in front of me as if watching a movie.

On my map I drew a tree with a small ladder coming up
out of the top of it to a cloud. I drew a bench and then a
rectangle with a line in it, like a notebook with a pen. I

drew a little swingset, and next to it a square and two little circles on top and a triangle on the side, an attempt at a movie camera.

I went on a run and thought about all the miles I'd run and all the words I'd written all summer. I thought about my newest essay and thought about my parents and my grandmother.

I kept running and I thought about Amber. I thought about all my friends. I thought about the summer and our temporary summer home and I thought about Tacoma and how magical it had all been.

I kept running and I didn't think about anything at all. The adrenaline or endorphins or dopamine or whatever kicked in like I'd snorted lines of Runner's High off the sexy flat stomach of the Puget Sound. My body felt bathtub warm all throughout and my brain tingled and tickled. I guess I kept running but really I was swimming but really I was floating but really I was getting a full body deep tissue massage while also it was all just more running.

Dude! Kevin said, putting an end to my massage and my levitating and my swim and my run.

Is this a dream? I said.

Kevin punched me square in the chest.

What the fuck, I said.

Proving you're awake, Kevin said.

Are you thinking of pinching? I said.

Kevin thought about that. Hm, he said. Maybe?

Punching or pinching, either way I guess it wasn't a dream. Though I wasn't sure what Kevin was doing in Tacoma.

What are you doing in Tacoma? I said.

Kevin laughed.

Dude, you're in Portland, Kevin said.

It did look different. I guess I thought that was what dream-Tacoma looked like.

What am I doing in Portland, I said?

Kevin told me I ran there which made me not-totally but half-remember running there.

That's like a hundred miles, I said.

A hundred-and-forty-three, Kevin said. Give or take. I don't know where exactly you left from.

Holy shit, I said. That's like five marathons. I've never even run one marathon.

Five and a half, Kevin said.

What time is it? I said.

Kevin looked up at the sky. 7:30, Kevin said.

Holy shit, I ran all night? I said.

I mean, you ran a hundred and forty-three miles, Kevin said.

That didn't really seem possible, but Kevin seemed like he knew what he was talking about.

I'm surprised I'm not more tired, I said. I'm starving though.

There's a great breakfast place just a few blocks away! Kevin said.

And then we walked one more mile, on top of the one hundred and forty-three, give or take, I'd just run, and got breakfast.

We got breakfast and then Kevin remembered it was adult soapbox derby day, so we got in his car and drove a bunch of roads that twisted and winded and seemed like a rollercoaster, until we were at some giant park in the woods.

We're here! Kevin said.

There were all these food carts and beer carts everywhere, so we started day drinking.

We spent the next few weeks watching bathtubs and arcade games and blow-up mattresses and NASCAR cars and giant stuffed animals and couches race each other through the cosmos.

Maybe this is the meaning of life? I realized, which felt honest and true. I reached into my back pocket to get my notebook so I wouldn't forget, but I didn't have a notebook with me and also I'd forgotten what the *this* was that I'd had in mind.

Let's go on a walk, a kangaroo said.

Sure, I said. Should we invite Kevin? I said, in a whisper.

I am Kevin, the kangaroo said.

OK, let's all go! I said.

The three of us went to the woods and went on a hike. We got lost and couldn't find our way out, and we had to sleep on beds of pine needles and survive on berries we foraged.

I'm really hungry for something other than berries, I finally said one day. And I miss my bed. And Amber.

Yeah, I get that, Kevin said. Let's go get some tacos and I'll drive you back up to Tacoma.

He led us out of the woods to his favorite taco place in town and then drove me back to Tacoma. He dropped me off and said he'd love to stay and hang out, but he really needed to get back home.

We should do that again soon though! Kevin said, and drove off.

I realized I'd never called Amber to tell her where I was, and then I remembered that I'd run five and a half marathons, all the way down to Portland, and that I'd spent weeks in a forest, living off the land, and I wasn't sure how to explain any of that to Amber, but when I walked in, she just asked me how my run was.

THE END

One morning we woke up and summer was over. Just like that. Time to return to our normal home and our normal lives and the normal world. We'd known it was coming, but we'd also been in denial.

We didn't end up completing our quest or objective or whatever because we never fully settled on anything and so didn't have one to complete.

I wrote a ton, but only short shorts and beginnings of longer stories and a couple essays and pages and pages of anecdotes and a few dumb jokes without punchlines. Not a word toward a novel. I ran a ton, though I had no mileage or number of runs or speed as a goal, so I didn't have a goal to hit. We had an infinite amount of fun, even more than we could have predicted, and that had more or less been Amber's goal, so maybe she completed hers.

We stood in the driveway together, staring at the house. The mirror image of when we'd arrived months before.

I thought about my buddy Bud Smith, and his story "Violets" that I sometimes teach that starts with a couple burning down their house. I thought of another buddy, Dave Housley, and his story collection *Massive Cleansing*

Fire, where every short story ends with, well, a massive fire. I thought about telling you, at the beginning of this very story, that this wouldn't be about the house being haunted or cursed or us ruining the place, and I thought about how sometimes stories are lies.

I think we should burn the house down, I said, like a joke, but also meaning it.

We should! Amber said. I couldn't tell if she was returning the joke or also meaning it or some secret third thing.

Let's do it, Amber said. Like in that one story by your buddy Bud. And also that story collection by Dave, she said.

I hadn't remembered telling her about those and was surprised she'd been paying attention and remembered whenever I had.

And also because you started this story by explicitly saying we wouldn't, Amber said.

I didn't know how she even knew about that.

We went inside and did one last walk through the house. It was empty, everything packed up ready to take home with us or thrown away. Except the giant map of Tacoma, still hanging on the wall in the room that had been my temporary summer office.

Hold on, Amber said. She carefully took the map down

off the wall and folded it and folded it again and again and again and again and again until it was the size of a mass market paperback, which she put in her back pocket.

OK, Amber said. Let's go.

We went to the door that said it was off limits. *No Muggles Allowed.* I reached into my pocket and grabbed the key that I didn't know but wasn't surprised was in there and unlocked the door. There was that pile of fireworks. There was that sign. *For later.*

I guess this is later? Amber said.

I guess so, I said.

We moved all the fireworks to the main room, shoving them into our pizza oven, all around it. Creating a giant inside bonfire of fireworks.

We went out to the house's backyard, which I haven't yet mentioned because we never really spent any time there, and there were a handful of gas cans, which I haven't yet mentioned because they hadn't previously existed. But they were there now.

We took the gas cans into the house and doused it all. Everything. We had a gasoline party. When everything was shiny wet and we started feeling high from the fumes, I grabbed two roman candles in one hand and Amber's hand in my other and we went outside.

In the driveway, I lit both roman candles and then handed one to Amber, and we both aimed and started shooting balls of fire into the windows we'd left open.

It started slow at first, nothing happening, and then a couple flames, and then all at once, the house lit up.

We stood in awe, watching flames lick and spark and paint the house orange and red and yellow and pink, and then all the fireworks starting going off, one here, one there, and then in quicker and quicker succession, a giant celebration of the whole burning down.

And then we got in the car and started driving to the airport.

Guilt pulled us into its undertow almost immediately.

I feel bad, Amber said.

Me too, I said.

We were barely blocks away, still in the neighborhood we'd gone on so many walks through the previous couple months. I could see the smoke and flames in my rearview mirror.

I don't think we should have done that, Amber said.

Yeah, probably we shouldn't have, I said.

It did look really badass though, Amber said.

She looked over at me and I did that thing characters in movies do all the time where I didn't give a shit about driving, I just looked at her. I could see the flames from behind us, bouncing off the rearview, reflected back at me in her eyes.

It really did, I said.

I leaned over toward her and she leaned toward me and we kissed, and then when we pulled away, Amber yelled at me to pay attention to the road.

I looked out ahead of us. I paid attention to the road.

And then I had an idea.

I have an idea, I said.

What are we doing? Amber said.

The mall! I said.

I can see that, Amber said. Why are we pulling into the mall?

You'll see, I said.

I drove to Macy's, because it was my favorite part of the mall when I was growing up, when it was the Bon Marche. There were columns everywhere, breaking up the big open space of the mall department store and spilling into the interior of the mall and around a water feature. I'd liked it because it was so different from everything else, and because it seemed fancy. It felt old and grand, reminding me of the Colosseum or the Parthenon and other buildings we'd studied and made models of in school. Now, I liked it because it was still different from everything else, and because it seemed fancy, but like my childhood idea of fancy. It still felt old and grand, but now that meant the 80s and its promise of commerce and adulthood, and like a Pacific Northwest version of a brutalist interpretation of ancient Roman and Greek empires.

No, but really, Amber said. What are you doing?

You'll see, I said again. I put the car in park, turned it off. Just trust me, I said.

Amber said she didn't trust me, though I knew she did, and got out of the car and followed.

We walked through the Macy's that used to be Bon Marche, out into the mall proper, past the Nordstrom that used to be Frederick & Nelson, or maybe it used to be Mervyn's, and past the Cinnabon and the Orange Julius and the Apple store that used to be KayBee Toys.

Spencer Gifts? Amber said, when I took her hand and pulled her into Spencer Gifts.

Trust me, I said again.

I'm starting to get a little scared, Amber said. Like a joke, but also meaning it.

That's fair, I said.

I kept hold of Amber's hand and pulled her past the cashier and past a bunch of novelty gifts and posters and candles and weird shit that I didn't even know what it was, all the way to the back of the store.

I moved the rack of t-shirts out of the way, and there behind them was a small door. Amber asked how I knew it was there and I reminded her that I'd told her to trust me, and smiled at her in a way that I thought was flirty and conspiratorial, but I'm not totally sure if that came through or not.

I discovered it that one day we came shopping together, when you were trying on jeans, I said.

OK? Amber said.

Yeah. So. You know. I was just killing time and I figured what the fuck, so I got in and followed it all the way to the end, I said.

What the fuck? Amber said.

I know! I said. What the fuck indeed. But that isn't even the what the fuck part. Get this. At the other end of the tunnel was my bedroom. Like, my childhood bedroom. From when I was a teenager. I was IN my childhood bedroom. But I wasn't just in my childhood bedroom. I was IN my childhood. Like, it was 1990.

What the fuck are you talking about? Amber said.

I know. I don't know. I can't explain it. Obviously. But that's what happened. Also, it might have actually been 1992. I don't know. Something like that.

I opened up the door, letting Amber see for herself.

It's like some kind of time-traveling tunnel to your child-hood, I said.

I looked at Amber and then looked into the tunnel along-side her. It didn't especially look like a time-traveling tun-nel to your childhood. Or maybe it did. I didn't have any idea what a time-traveling tunnel to your childhood was supposed to look like.

C'mon, I said. I got down on all fours and started crawling.

TIME-TRAVELING TUNNEL TO YOUR CHILDHOOD

What happened was, I crawled and crawled and crawled and crawled and crawled and then, at the end of the tunnel was another door, and when I opened that and crawled through, just like the last time, I was right back in my childhood bedroom.

I looked behind me and Amber wasn't there. The tunnel was so small, I hadn't had any space to turn around and check for her while I'd been crawling. I'd assumed she was there. She was probably there? I had no idea at what point she'd stopped being there.

I was looking into the tunnel confused, looking for Amber, wondering if I'd lost her somewhere along the way or she'd never followed me into the tunnel to begin with or what, and the door closed. And then disappeared.

There was nothing where the door had been, just a second before. Just like that.

What the fuck?

The Idea Hadn't Really Been Thought Through

That was pretty classic me. Amber was always giving me shit for that.

Amber had said she wished we hadn't lit our temporary summer home on fire, and I'd wished we hadn't too, and it turned out I knew this time traveling tunnel, and so I figured we could time travel back to before we lit the house on fire. Easy peasy! Problem, meet solution!

I hadn't thought about how I didn't really understand any of the rules or logistics of the time traveling tunnel. Or that last time it had taken me all the way back to 1990. Or 1992. Or something like that. I hadn't thought about what it might mean to bring Amber to my childhood or if she would come out the tunnel into her own childhood bedroom or what.

Wait, was that where she'd gone? Was she in her own childhood bedroom? In her own past?

I hadn't really thought through any of it. Which, like I said, is very much one of the very things Amber was always giving me shit about.

A storm of exhaustion flash-flooded my body, and I moved to the bed and the room went dark and I fell asleep.

1992

Just like last time, I slept for a lifetime. Just like last time, my parents woke me up in the morning. My dad said he made pancakes and my mom said to hurry up, it was her turn for carpool. Just like last time, I woke up and I ate pancakes and I went back to my bedroom to get dressed.

Unlike last time, the secret door was no longer there.

I couldn't open that secret door and get in, couldn't crawl and crawl and crawl and crawl until I found the door at the other end, couldn't return to Spencer Gifts, just like that.

Couldn't do anything but get dressed and go to school, best I could tell.

I got dressed and went to school.

After school, I got home and went straight to my bedroom, hoping the secret door would be there again. It wasn't. I went through the rest of the evening the same as I had the first time around, back in 1992, which is where I now was. When I now was? My mom made dinner, and then we all watched *Wonder Years* together; I went to my room and listened to my radio and read a little *Beckett Baseball Card Monthly* until my parents came in and told me it was bed time.

The next day I did more or less the same. And then again the day after that, and the day after that, and the day after that, etc. etc. etc.

I lived being 14 again, and then it was my birthday and we went to a Tacoma Tigers game to celebrate, and then I was 15 and I lived that again.

The secret door to the time-traveling tunnel to take me back to the future and being an adult never reappeared.

I made sure to wear sunscreen every time I went out in the sun. I drank more water. I thought about trying to make myself like running, but then I remembered that part of what I loved about running in my 40s was that it was new to my 40s, so I went back to hating running, just like I had the first time through.

I lived my life the second time through almost the same as I had the first time. *Almost.*

I kissed the girl I went out on a date with when I was sixteen who I'd wanted to kiss my first life through but had been too shy to initiate. I'd always thought that if I'd kissed we would have gone out on a second date, maybe kept dating, but she and still-me didn't go out again same as old-her and old-me hadn't, so that proved that wrong.

I was a little nicer to my parents, without even meaning or trying to be, because I knew how much adult-me appreciated them. Still only a little though. I was still a teenager. I told my grandmother how much I loved and appreciated her for the same reason.

I was scared of doing anything different and what that might mean, how it might change things, and also I was still just me and still-me was more or less the same as old-me. More or less.

Little by little, I recognized my life and the world around me less and less. Every little change created little ripples, washing me further and further away from the shore of old-me.

I went to grad school two years after undergrad instead of seven.

I moved back to Tacoma after grad school.

I saved my money and I invested it… let's call it *wisely*. I'd promised myself I'd never use my time-traveling knowledge in any unfair ways, but then I convinced myself it wasn't unfair to spoil myself a little as a tradeoff for having lived this life twice.

Every time I met an Eric, I'd ask if he had a co-worker named Amber, or a sister-in-law Rachel; and every time I met a Richie, I'd ask if he had a cousin, Jessie, or a hair-stylist, Jesse; and every time I met an Arthur, I'd asked if he was writing any new stories; and every time I met a Georgie, I'd ask if he was *from* any stories; and every time I met a Ted and/or Alice, I'd ask if they happened to own a beautiful home they were looking for a housesitter for the summer for.

I kept an eye on real estate listings, and when I saw a list-ing for a beautiful mid-century modern style house with a main room with a wall of windows that looked out at the Puget Sound and the Olympic Mountains in the background, and a giant wraparound deck that, on one side, looked out at that same view of the Puget Sound with the Olympic Mountains in the background, and around on the other side, a view that looked out at Mount Rainier, I bought it.

I spent my days marveling at the view and enjoying this life I'd made for myself.

I bought TV on the Radio's *Seeds* and The National's *Sleep Well Beast* and Cave In's *Heavy Pendulum* when they were released, listened to them on my record player in my music-listening-room, surrounded by three walls of built-in bookshelves, two of which were filled with books and the third with records.

And then one day there was a knock on my door.

The Map of Tacoma

I opened the door and Amber stood there.

I stared at her. She stared back at me.

She looked the same, but different.

You look the same, but different, she said.

I smiled. I was thinking the same about you, I said.

You sound the same too, Amber said. She'd always lovingly made fun of my raspy voice.

We hugged and we kissed and we made out.

How'd you find me? I finally said.

What do you mean? Amber said. She gestured around the house, like, *duh*.

I looked around at old-us's-temporary-summer-house-turned-new-me's-current-house.

Sure, I said. Sure, sure.

But also because of this, Amber said.

She reached back and took a paperback out of her back pocket. And then unfolded it, and then unfolded again, and again and again and again and again and again.

And then, all unfolded on the ground all around us, was the map I'd drawn from my first playthrough.

Remember what I said? Amber said.

I remembered lots of things she said but had no idea which thing she meant.

Remember when I stared at this map and asked how we beat it? Amber said.

Our quest! I said.

We beat it, Amber said.

Holy shit, I said. I forgot about it.

We kissed again and then held hands and toured the house, same as we had once upon a time.

The kitchen; the two bathrooms; the spare bedroom I never used for anything; the couple walk-in closets; another office that I never used but now maybe Amber could, if she ever needed or wanted to; the laundry room; the loft I also never really used but loved having, I liked the idea and the sound of it, *loft*; the study with a big, comfy chair like for reading in, and three walls of built-in bookshelves, two of which were filled with books but the third was full of records, and in the corner was a stereo and record player, which I thought of as my "music-listening-room"; and one locked door that I had no idea what was on the other side of.

You locked this door to make it like before? Amber said.

I shook my head. It was locked when I bought the house, I said.

And you've never unlocked it? Amber said.

I don't have the key, I said. I shrugged. And I kind of like the mystery of it, I guess, I said.

No adjustable height desk?! Amber yelled when we got to the room that was my primary office.

Yeah, I said. I wanted to say more but wasn't sure what.

We should get one, Amber said. Next time we go to Costco! Amber said.

You can sit at it—or stand at it, whatever—and write about all this! Amber said. This could be your Great Tacoma Novel.

I didn't think I'd ever told her about that.

You never told me, Amber said. But I knew.

Of course she did.

And this, right now, this very moment could be the end! I said.

I'd never known the end of something before I started before. It was exciting. Maybe that was what I needed to write a novel. It didn't really matter if it was great or Tacoma or Pacific Northwest or American or Great. I mostly just wanted it to be fun and stupid and inventive, but earnest and nostalgic and open-hearted too.

Amber pulled me out onto the wraparound porch. We looked together out at the water and the mountains and all the trees.

It looked and felt like a postcard. Like we were living inside a single perfect shot from a movie. Like my nostalgic heart spilled out on canvas and come alive.

Remember what I said that first night out here? Amber said.

Give me a hint, I said.

Amber leaned into my ear and whispered. There was no need, it was only us two, but whispering it was sexier.

Remember? Amber said, conspiratorial and flirty.

And I remembered.

And that's the end.

Acknowledgments

Thank you to all my friends and family in and around Tacoma, who mostly don't appear in this Tacoma but who make my real Tacoma so magical and special.

Thank you to my writing group buddies, Matt Kirkpatrick and Russ Brakefield.

Thank you to Barrelhouse's WriterCamp, where I wrote a big chunk of this.

Thank you to all the editors who published portions of this in literary journals — everyone at *Jake*, Mike McClelland at *Bluestem,* Kevin Maloney and Ryan-Ashley (Anderson) Maloney at *Pool Party,* Joshua Hebburn at *X-R-A-Y.*

Thank you to the gang at Autofocus — Sienna Zeilinger for the smart eye and great edits, Amy Wheaton for the amazing cover, and Michael Wheaton for loving this book and building a press that is so special and I am so excited to call home.

Thank you to Amber, for making our summer in Tacoma and this book and my life so magical and special and fun.

Aaron Burch grew up in Tacoma, WA.

The Dead Dad Diaries — Erin Slaughter

A Revionist History of Loving Men — Lena Ziegler

Marginalia — Naomi Washer

The Third Beat — Lauren Lavín

Teen Queen Training: Essays after The Seventeen Book of Etiquette and Entertaining, 1963 — Kristine Langley Mahler